Contents

CHAPTER 1

A Christmas Gift

It was a cold and snowy Christmas Eve. The March sisters were all gathered around the fire, knitting. They didn't feel very festive, since their father was away in the war, and there was no money for presents.

"It would be so lovely to have some pretty things," said Meg, the oldest.

"Who needs pretty things?" scoffed Jo, the second oldest. "I would like a thrilling new book to read."

Little Amy, the youngest, sighed dramatically. "Oh, what I wouldn't give for some new drawing pencils!"

"I would wish for some lovely new piano music," said quiet Beth, "but we mustn't fuss. We must try to be good and kind, like Marmee." Marmee was their pet name for their mother, who was out visiting the poor in their town.

"You're so right, Beth," said Jo. "After all, we have warmth and good company."

"And delicious food," added Amy.

By the time Marmee came home, the sisters were as happy as ever. They all sang carols around Beth's tiny piano and went up to bed, excited for the next day.

When the girls woke on Christmas morning, Marmee was already out visiting the Hummels, a poor family who lived nearby. The girls prepared their Christmas breakfast of warm bread, pancakes, and cream. When Marmee came home, she told them that the Hummels had no food at all.

"We should give the Hummel family our breakfast," said Beth, and the other girls agreed.

"I knew you would say that." Marmee smiled at them. "You are kind girls."

That evening, the sisters performed a Christmas play for all their friends. Jo had written it and played the dashing hero. They had so much fun that they barely thought about all the things their Christmas lacked. When Marmee called them all to dinner, they were surprised to see that it was a feast! There was cake, fruit, bonbons, and even ice cream!

"Did fairies do this?" asked Amy.

Marmee laughed. "No, Mr. Laurence sent it when he heard what you did for the Hummels."

The girls had often glimpsed rich old Mr. Laurence and his young grandson in the big house next door, and thought they looked nice but lonely.

"Maybe now we can make friends with them," Jo said.

On New Year's Eve, Jo and Meg went to a party. Meg was looking forward to dressing up in their prettiest frocks, until she saw that Jo's dress had a big burn mark on the back.

"You always stand too close to the fire," sighed Meg, feeling sad that they couldn't afford new clothes. "You'll just have to keep your back to the wall."

The party was beautiful, and Meg was asked to dance at once. Jo decided to hide in the library, so nobody would see her burnt dress.

She slipped inside—and bumped straight into the Laurence boy!

Jo remembered her manners. "Mr. Laurence, I must thank you for the Christmas feast you sent us," she said.

The boy laughed. "Please, call me

Laurie, and it was all Grandfather's idea."

"In that case, call me Jo, and I bet you told him to," said Jo.

Laurie was just as nice as Jo had hoped. Soon, they were chatting like old pals and doing silly dances where nobody could see.

After the party, Laurie walked Jo and Meg back home, and the sisters hoped that they had made a new friend.

One cold day, Jo was clearing snow outside, when she caught sight of Laurie watching her from an upstairs window. He looked a little sorry for himself.

Jo knew it wasn't ladylike, but she cupped her hands and shouted up anyway. "What's wrong?"

Laurie opened the window. "I've got a cold, so I have to stay inside. It's so dull."

"Well, why don't I come over and cheer you up?" said Jo.

"Would you?" Laurie asked.

"Of course!" said Jo. "I'll just ask Marmee."

A few minutes later, the doorbell rang. Laurie dashed downstairs to find Jo on the doorstep with some strange bundles.

"When I told them you were sick, Marmee sent her love, Meg sent her blancmange, and Beth sent her kittens," Jo said, giggling as one of the kittens tried to wriggle free.

"That's so kind of them," said Laurie. "Do come in."

They played with the kittens for a while, and then Laurie gave Jo a tour of the house. Jo enjoyed seeing where he lived, even though fine things didn't mean much to her. But when they reached the enormous library, she was speechless! There were hundreds of books. Jo spun around, gazing at them dreamily.

Down the hallway, they heard the heavy creak of the front door opening.

Laurie said, "That's the doctor. I'll be back in a minute."

Jo explored the library and stopped in front of a grand painting of an old gentleman. It was Mr. Laurence, Laurie's grandfather.

When she heard Laurie come back in, she said, "Your grandfather isn't as handsome as my grandfather, but he looks kind. I think I like him."

"Thank you, ma'am," said a gruff voice behind her.

Jo turned in horror to see Mr. Laurence standing there. She stammered an apology, but the old man waved it off, smiling.

"Now, what are you doing in my library?" he asked.

"I thought Laurie looked lonely, sir. I came to cheer him up," Jo said nervously, still feeling like she was on thin ice.

Mr. Laurence looked thoughtful. "Lonely, you say? Well, perhaps it wouldn't hurt for him to have a bit of company, and you seem like a nice girl."

To Jo's surprise, he invited her to tea and said that the March girls were welcome to visit whenever they liked.

CHAPTER 2

Shyness and Pride

Jo, Meg, and Amy did as Mr. Laurence said. They were often in and out of the big house, and it became full of life and laughter. However, Beth was too shy to go over, even though she dreamed about the Laurences' grand piano.

Mr. Laurence decided to try to help Beth. He staged a loud chat with Marmee, making sure Beth would overhear.

"It's such a shame. The grand piano sits alone at the far end of the house. Laurie is away upstairs, and I'm shut in my study all day.

Nobody would even hear if it was played. I would be very grateful if one of your girls would. They can just let themselves in and out."

That day, Beth went over to the big house and slipped in through the side  door. She found the piano alone, as promised, and started to play. She had a wonderful time, playing for hours. Then, she closed the lid and ran home, absolutely thrilled.

She started to creep over every day, and she had no idea that Mr. Laurence was sitting with his study door open, or that Laurie was sneaking down to the hall to listen to the sweet tunes she played.

Beth made Mr. Laurence some slippers, as a gift to say thank you for letting her play his piano, and left them in his study.

To begin with, Beth heard nothing from him and was worried that he was offended by the small present. Then, one day, when she was coming home from a walk, she saw her sisters waving out of the window like crazy.

"Beth! It's a letter from Mr. Laurence," said Amy, waving a piece of paper. "You'll never guess what he's sent you!"

Beth ran inside to find the whole family standing around a little cabinet piano. Mr. Laurence's letter said that he loved her gift, and he wanted to give her something in return.

Beth sat down on the stool in a daze and touched the keys. It sounded beautiful!

"You'd better go and thank him," joked Jo, knowing that Beth would be too shy.

But to everyone's surprise, Beth jumped straight up. "Yes, I suppose I should."

She marched next door, ran in, and gave Mr. Laurence a big hug.

Her sisters were shocked when they heard this.

"I do declare the world is coming to an end!" said Meg.

Amy was the only sister who still went to school. Beth was too shy and did her lessons at home. Meg and Jo had both finished school and had jobs. Meg was a governess for a rich family. Jo went to read for their Great Aunt March and keep her company.

"Oh, dear me, it is so terrible to be in debt," Amy sighed as she, Jo, and Meg left the house one morning.

"Debt? What do you mean?" Meg asked.

"I owe at least a dozen pickled limes at school," Amy said, in a weary voice.

 "And I have no money to buy any. Jenny Snow is calling me mean behind my back."

Meg nodded seriously. She remembered how she had always wanted to join in on the latest fashions at school herself. "How much money do you need?"

"A quarter," said Amy.

Meg pulled one out of her purse. "Just make this last as long as you can. We don't have a lot of money," she warned.

Amy was late to school that day, but word quickly went around the class that she had twenty-four delicious  limes. Amy promised to share them with everyone, except for nasty Jenny Snow.

What Amy hadn't told Meg was that Mr. Davis, her teacher, had banned pickled limes from school. So, when Jenny Snow raised her hand and told him that Amy had a bag of them in her desk, he was furious.

He ordered Amy to throw the limes out of the window. Slowly and sadly, Amy did as he said. Next, he made her stand

at the front of the classroom and hold out her hands. Mr. Davis struck her hands three times with a leather strap, then ordered her to stand on the platform until recess. Her hands stung a lot, but Amy was determined not to cry. She stood there silently.

When the bell rang, she ran to the cloakroom. She gathered her things and ran out of school, vowing never to go back.

When she got home and told her family what had happened, they were furious that she had been struck. Marmee said it was wrong to have broken the rules, but she didn't believe in hitting children. She wrote a letter to Mr. Davis, telling him that Amy would do her lessons at home with Beth from now on.

One evening, Jo, Meg, and Laurie were going to see a play. Amy had been stuck inside with a cold for the past few days and was bored.

"Please, can I come, too?" she asked as the older two got ready.

"Marmee says you aren't well enough yet," said Meg. "You can go next week with Beth."

Amy pouted. "But it won't be nearly as fun with Beth. Please, Meg, I'm dying for some fun."

Meg looked thoughtfully at Jo. "I suppose if we bundle her up …"

"No," said Jo firmly. "She wasn't invited."

"But Meg says I can, and I'll pay for myself," Amy said. She started to pull on her boots, happy that she was going to get her way.

"No," said Jo. "We already have tickets, so your seat will be somewhere else. You know that Laurie will give you his seat, and he will sit alone. So, you will be ruining his evening and mine. You aren't coming, and that's that!"

Laurie called from downstairs, and Meg and Jo dashed down.

Just as they were on their way out of the door, Amy yelled over the banisters, "You'll be sorry for this, Jo March!"

CHAPTER 3

Anger and Vanity

Jo returned from the evening out and ran straight upstairs to write. She had been working on a little book of fairy tales for the last year that she hoped to finish before Father got home.

But the book wasn't where she had left it. She went downstairs and asked if anyone had seen it.

A guilty look passed over Amy's face.

"Give it back, Amy, " Jo demanded.

 "I can't. You'll never see your silly book again," said Amy.

"Why not?"

"I burned it up,"

Amy said. "I told you you would be sorry for leaving me behind!"

Jo burst into tears and shook Amy hard. "You are a wicked girl. I'll never forgive you for as long as I live!"

She raced from the room, sobbing, ran upstairs, and hurled herself down on her bed.

If Amy had expected the rest of the family to side with her, she was disappointed. They all agreed it had been a terrible thing to do.

Amy crept up to Jo's room later that night. "Jo, I'm sorry. Please forgive me."

Jo didn't even look at her. "I will never forgive you. You don't deserve it."

Jo was in a bad mood for days. Nothing could make her feel better, because nothing could bring her book back. Amy tried to show Jo that she was sorry, but it was no use. Eventually, Jo decided to get out of the house and go ice skating with Laurie.

Amy heard the clash of skates as Jo was getting ready to leave. She turned to Meg. "Jo promised me that the next time she went ice skating, I could come, too. I bet she'll go back on that promise now."

"You did do a dreadful thing, Amy. I'm not surprised that Jo finds it hard to forgive you," Meg said. "But I think she might, if you wait until the right moment. Why don't you follow her and wait until Laurie has put her in a good mood? Then, you can sneak up to her and give her a kiss. I'm sure all will be forgotten."

Amy thought that was an excellent idea and hurried to get ready.

Out on the icy river, Jo heard Amy following and rolled her eyes. Laurie glanced back, but before he could say anything, Jo muttered, "Ignore her. She just wants attention, and she won't have mine."

Laurie skated ahead, around the river bend. "The ice is getting a little thin in the middle here, Jo," he called back. "Better keep to the edge to be safe."

Jo skated to the edge of the river. She thought briefly about calling back to Amy but then shrugged. "She came by herself, so she can look out for herself."

 A moment after Jo rounded the bend, she heard a great crack, a scream, and a splash. She and Laurie raced back to see Amy gasping and thrashing in a hole in the ice.

All of Jo's anger disappeared like a melting snowflake. She shot toward her little sister. She and Laurie pulled Amy out and rushed her home, wrapped in their coats.

At home, Amy warmed up again and was no worse for wear.

While she slept in front of the fire, Jo admitted what she did to Marmee and began to sob. "How can I control my terrible temper, Marmee?" she cried. "Amy could have died, and it would have been my fault!"

Marmee hugged her. "It's something you need to work on, dear, and there's no shame in it. Many people need to work on it their entire lives."

One spring day, the house was full of excitement. Meg had been invited to stay with her friend, Annie Moffat. The Moffat family were going to throw a party while Meg was there, so all the March sisters were helping Meg mend and pack her best things. They knew they were poor, but they didn't want Meg to feel ashamed of her clothes. Marmee even opened her "treasure chest," which was where she kept her few nice things left from before they were poor. She gave Meg silk stockings, a new sash, and a pretty fan.

Meg left in high spirits, but when she arrived at the party, she felt dowdy next to the other girls. Annie and her sisters were kind, even if they thought too much about what they looked like, and they offered to lend Meg a brand-new party dress.

When Meg accepted, they decided to transform her looks too. They crimped and curled her hair, brushed her skin with powder, and painted her lips. Then, they added necklaces, bracelets, gloves, and even silk boots.

When they were finished, Meg did look very pretty but like a doll instead of her own natural self.

At the party, everyone admired Meg, especially the men. Meg knew she was too young for boys, but she couldn't help enjoying the attention. She flirted and drank champagne, until she saw Laurie over on the other side of the room.

Meg glided over. "Laurie! I didn't know you were going to be here! Shall we dance?"

Laurie frowned a little as he looked at her. "You look … odd."

It was Meg's turn to frown. "Don't you mean I look nice?"

Laurie shook his head. "I don't mean to be rude, Meg, but you don't look like you. You look like one of those silly girls who only care about their looks."

Meg caught a glimpse of herself in a mirror and suddenly felt very ashamed. Laurie was right, she thought. She wasn't behaving like herself at all.

When the party was over, Meg went home to confess to Marmee what she had done.

"Wanting to look nice once in a while is fine," Marmee soothed her. "It's only a problem when it's all you think about."

"Well, I shan't worry about my looks from now on," Meg vowed. "I want to be more than that."

CHAPTER 4

All Play and No Work

The girls had many fun games that they would play together. These helped to fill the evenings after work, lessons, and chores were done for the day. When it was cold and dark outside, the little house was warm, bright, and full of joy.

Once a week, the girls would go up to the attic and dress up as characters from a book called *The Pickwick Papers* by Charles Dickens. All the characters were quaint English gentlemen. As these characters, the girls had formed the Pickwick Club.

"I, Augustus Snodgrass, call this meeting to order!" said Jo, straightening her top hat.

"You can't do that," said Meg, peering over a huge pair of spectacles with no glass

in them. "I'm the president! I, Samuel Pickwick, call this meeting to order. Mr. Tupman, do you have the newsletter?"

Beth handed over a bundle of papers. They all wrote pieces for the newsletter each week, which included stories, poems, recipes, news, and anything else they could think to write about.

Meg opened up the paper. "We shall begin with a note from Nathaniel Winkle." She nodded at Amy.

Once all the notices had been read out, Jo bounced to her feet. "I say, girls— I mean, gentlemen—I have an idea. Why don't we add a new member to the club? Someone you all like and who is ever so jolly and fun. Let Laurie join the club!"

There was silence.

Then Meg said, "I don't think that's a good idea, Mr. Snodgrass. Of course we all like Laurie, but he'll think this club is silly and make fun of us."

"Oh, let him join!" Jo pleaded. "He won't make fun of us. He'll join in, I know he will. Besides," she added sheepishly, "he's already here."

She flung open the door of the closet, and Laurie jumped out. Meg, Beth, and Amy all fell off their chairs in surprise.

"I'm sorry to shock you!" Laurie laughed. "I'm afraid it was all my idea, and I persuaded Snodgrass. My name is Samuel Weller."

And so, Laurie joined the Pickwick Club and proved to be an excellent member. He even set up an old birdhouse between their houses, which served as a mailbox so they could exchange letters and small presents.  Laurie threw himself into character and wrote lots of funny pieces. Every week, the Marches' attic would ring with laughter late into the evening.

That summer, the girls felt that they had worked so hard, they deserved some time off. Meg and Jo decided not to go to work, while Beth and Amy abandoned their lessons.

"Although, it won't be a complete rest if we still have to do our chores," said Amy to Marmee, hopefully.

"That's true," said Marmee, "but you might find that you will feel bored and unhappy if you have nothing to do."

The girls couldn't possibly believe that was true. So Marmee suggested they spend a whole week doing nothing—with no chores—and see how they felt at the end.

"I think we'll have a fabulous time," said Jo.

The experiment was agreed, and each girl set out to do whatever she pleased.

The week wasn't as enjoyable as the girls had hoped. Meg decided to alter one of her old dresses. But she couldn't resist fiddling with it over and over. By the time she was finished with it, it was ruined.

Jo went out rowing with Laurie in the blazing sun for hours, and her nose got sunburned. Then she gave herself a headache by reading too much.

Meanwhile, Beth decided she would clean out her doll cupboard, tidy all their clothes, and brush their hair. But she got bored halfway through and decided she would rather play piano instead. She left the dolls all over the floor, where everybody tripped over them.

Amy discovered that she didn't have much imagination by herself. She couldn't think of anything fun to do and ended up sitting on the window seat, staring outside.

On the evening of the third day, Marmee asked them how they were all feeling about their experiment.

There was silence for a moment, and then Jo exploded. "It's awful. I hate having nothing to do!"

The other girls agreed.

Marmee smiled at them all. "I knew you would feel that way," she said. "It's only by having work and chores that we truly enjoy our time off to play and dream. And now you have learned that for yourselves."

The girls agreed that they definitely had. They were all ready to throw themselves back into work, and Jo knew just what she was going to work on …

A few days later, Jo was writing in the attic, when she suddenly put down her pen.

"That's it, then," she said to herself.

She shuffled the paper into a stack and tied it with a red ribbon.  Then, she slipped on her coat and hat, picked up the paper, and set off into town, without telling anyone where she was going. In town,

she disappeared into some offices for an hour. When she came out, Laurie was across the street.

He hurried over. "Hello, Jo. What brings you to town?"

Jo looked flushed but proud as she replied. "I finished my book."

"Jo, that's splendid! Well done!" cried Laurie.

"Thank you," said Jo. "I took it to the newspaper offices. The editor says that they might print a couple of my stories next week. I won't tell the others yet, in case it doesn't happen."

Laurie was so proud of his friend, he felt that he might burst. They were very giggly when they got back from town, and nobody knew why they both took a sudden interest in reading the newspaper …

CHAPTER 5
Dark Days

One day, Jo was looking through the newspaper while her sisters sewed.

"There's a story here," Jo said, casually. "Shall I read it to you?"

"Go on, then," said Meg.

Jo cleared her throat. "The story is called *The Rival Painters.*"

The tale was about two painters who both loved the same woman. They competed for her by each trying to paint the most beautiful picture.

"What a wonderful love story!" Meg exclaimed at the end.

"I thought the painting parts were the best," said Amy.

Beth asked, "Who wrote it?"

Jo paused for a moment and blushed.
"I did."

All of her sisters leaped up to hug her,
and Marmee couldn't have been prouder.

Jo explained that she wouldn't be paid
for this story because she was a beginner,
but the newspaper would pay for the next
one. One day, she hoped to make enough
money to support herself and the girls.

"You have used your talents well," said
Marmee. "Father will be pleased, Jo."

It was a grim November day when a telegram was delivered for Marmee. Everybody froze. Telegrams were only used for emergencies. Marmee opened it and then cried out in shock and sorrow. It read: *Mrs. March. Come at once. Your husband is in a hospital in Washington. He is very ill.*

All the girls broke down in tears, sobbing, and Marmee turned as white as a sheet.

Marmee asked Laurie to send a return telegram, saying she would come at once. She sent Jo to town to buy medicine and asked Meg and Amy to help her pack. She told Beth to go next door and ask

Mr. Laurence if he would watch over the girls while she was gone.

All the girls hurried to obey.

Beth returned from the Laurences' with Mr. Brooke, Laurie's tutor.

"Mr. Laurence has business in Washington that he wants me to see to," Mr. Brooke explained. "So, I thought we could travel together."

Marmee knew that Mr. Laurence didn't really have business in Washington, and Mr. Brooke was just coming to help her.

"Thank you so much," she smiled. "That is very kind of you."

Jo took a very long time to come back from town and Marmee was starting to worry when she walked in, still wearing her bonnet and cape.

Jo went straight to Marmee and put down a small roll of dollar bills. "Here, Marmee, this is for making Father better and bringing him home."

Mrs. March picked up the money. "This is twenty-five dollars, Jo! Wherever did you get such money?"

Jo's voice wobbled a little. "It's all mine. I didn't beg, borrow, or steal it, and I don't think you can be cross with me, for I sold something that was all mine."

As she spoke, she pulled off her bonnet. All of her beautiful long hair had been chopped off!

"JO!" her family cried. They all crowded

around asking why she had done such a thing. Jo's hair was beautiful, and she had been so proud of it.

"I wanted to do something to help Father," said Jo stoutly. "I was walking past the barbershop in town, and I saw that they bought hair, so I knew that was it. I don't regret it at all, if it helps Father."

Marmee hugged Jo. "You are a good girl," she whispered.

The next morning, the girls were tired and pale as they got up. They had all been too worried about Father to sleep much. When Marmee appeared from her room, it was obvious that she hadn't slept at all.

"We mustn't cry in front of Marmee," Meg whispered to her sisters. "We must be brave."

But it was hard. Amy's lips wobbled a few times during breakfast, and Jo had to leave the room.

Nobody was really eating anything anyway.

Soon, it was time for Marmee to leave. She hugged each of her daughters in turn, reminding them to be good and to visit the Hummel family for her while she was gone. Mr. Laurence had agreed to watch over the girls while Marmee

was away. He and Laurie came out to
wave as she left.

The girls gave Marmee their messages
of love for Father. Then, Marmee climbed
into the carriage with Mr. Brooke and set
off. She turned back to wave at her girls
and blow one last kiss.

The girls managed weak smiles

until the carriage had
rounded the corner,
and then they all
burst into tears
and hugged each
other for comfort.

The girls did their best to be good, like Marmee asked, but it was difficult when they were so worried about Father. They all did their chores, but Meg, Jo, and Amy didn't go to visit the Hummels once.

Faithful Beth visited every day, taking food. But she grew worried; the Hummels' baby was sick, and she didn't know what to do for it. Still, she would put on her little cape every day and trudge down the lane, trying to help.

One evening, Jo found her curled up on the floor next to Marmee's medicine cabinet, shivering.

"Why, Beth, what is the matter?" Jo cried.

"The baby had scarlet fever," Beth whimpered. "I think I have it too. I've taken some medicine. You and Meg both had it already, didn't you?"

"Yes," Jo said. "We had scarlet fever
as children, so we won't get it again,
but Amy hasn't had it. We'll have to
send her to Aunt March's. Oh, this is
all my fault! I should have gone to the
Hummels, but I was too lazy! Well, I
won't be too lazy to nurse you. Come on,
Beth. Let's get you to bed."

CHAPTER 6

A New Dawn

Jo had hoped that Beth wouldn't have the fever badly, but she was bitterly disappointed. Beth got very sick. She couldn't eat or drink and drifted in and out of bad dreams. Half the time, she didn't even seem to know who Jo was.

To begin with, Jo was determined not to tell Marmee. She had to take care of Father, and it would be no good worrying her, when Beth would be better by the time she was home anyway. But Beth did not improve. If anything, she got worse.

One day, Jo slipped out of the darkened bedroom, with tears running down her face. Meg and Laurie were in the hall.

Jo took a deep breath. "I think we should send a message to Marmee. She needs to come back home because poor Beth is so sick. Laurie, could you go to town and send a message?"

Laurie blushed. "Actually, I already sent a telegram this morning. I talked to Grandfather, and he agreed that it was the right thing to do. I hope you don't mind."

Jo stared at him for a moment in disbelief. Then, she threw her arms around him. "Oh, thank you, Laurie, thank you! Marmee will know what to do."

Beth got worse and worse that night. In the dark, moonlit hours she lay so still, it almost looked like she was dead, except for the sweat on her face.

Jo never left her bedside. "Beth, please don't die," she whispered over and over again as she held Beth's hot little hand.

Nobody in the family slept that night. Not Meg, pacing up and down in the hallway. Not Amy, kneeling at the window at Aunt March's. Not Marmee, racing back home through the darkness. Not Father, left behind in Washington, getting better but still fragile. None of them could believe that the sweetest and kindest of them all might be taken so soon.

A lamp blazed all night in the Laurence house, too, as Laurie and his grandfather prayed for Beth.

Around dawn, Beth's fever seemed to break. Her face relaxed, and she breathed easily. The doctor arrived and said that she was getting better. Jo knelt down by the bed and said a prayer of thanks. The morning light shone through the window and down onto Beth. As Jo looked up, Marmee appeared in the doorway, and she knew all would be well.

Beth's recovery put everyone in the best mood for Christmas. She was still weak and had to be wrapped in blankets, carried from place to place. But she was talking and smiling again, bearing her illness with a cheerfulness that only she could have.

The morning of Christmas Day dawned bright and sunny. There had been fresh snow overnight, so everything gleamed pure white.

Marmee's present to Beth was a red dressing gown made of the softest wool. Beth immediately asked for it to be put on, and she looked like a festive elf! Then, Marmee carried her over to the

window to see
the rest of
her presents.

In the white
garden outside
stood a beautiful
snow sculpture
of a lady. She
was wearing a crown of holly and had
a bright new blanket draped around
her shoulders. In one hand, she held a
basket full of beautiful fruit and flowers.
In the other, she held a roll of piano
music. She looked so funny that Beth
laughed out loud!

Jo and Laurie sang Christmas carols
through the window. Then, they
presented Beth with each of their gifts,
and her laughter turned to tears of joy.

"I'm so full of happiness, if Father was here, I couldn't hold one drop more," said Beth, gazing around at all her beautiful gifts.

The other girls all agreed and knew that they were very lucky to have such wonderful presents and to spend a lovely day together.

Shortly after that, when Beth had gone to have her nap, Laurie stuck his head around the door. "Here's another present for the March family."

He stepped aside to reveal Mr. Brooke leading a tall man who was muffled up in scarves and overcoats.

"FATHER!"

There was a stampede as the entire family seemed to lose their minds at once and rushed toward Mr. March. He was invisible under all the hugs. Jo almost fainted from shock and happiness, while

Amy tripped over a footstool in her mad
dash and ended up hugging Father's legs.

A little too late, Marmee said,"Hush
now, we'll wake Beth."

But as she spoke, the study door was
flung open, and they heard a shriek of
excitement. Beth appeared in her little
red dressing gown. With a strength she
hadn't had in months, she ran straight
into her father's arms.

Christmas dinner was the merriest anybody could ever remember. The Laurences and Mr. Brooke joined them, and Father and Beth sat in armchairs at the head of the table together. There was a delicious golden-brown turkey with all the trimmings and a plum pudding afterward.

They drank to each other's health, sang songs, and shared stories of their year. The girls and Laurie had planned to go on a sleigh ride, but they called it off. None of the March girls wanted to leave their father's side.

As dusk fell, the Laurences and Mr. Brooke went home, leaving the March family sitting by the fire.

"Do you remember, girls, a year ago we were all gathered around feeling miserable about Christmas without Father?" asked Jo.

"I do," said Meg, "but I think it's been quite a nice year overall."

"It's been a difficult one," said Amy.

"Yes, but now Father is home," said Beth, nuzzling into him.

Mr. March smiled around at his family. "It has been a difficult year at times for all of us, but I'm so proud of my girls. You are growing into fine young women."

The girls all sat up, their eyes shining.

"Really, Father?" Meg asked.

"Yes, my dear," he replied. "I see that you are not vain anymore, that Jo is becoming more ladylike, that Beth has been brave, and that Amy is not so proud. Nobody is perfect, but we must all work toward being better every day, and that is what you do." He smiled around at them all.

In that moment, the March sisters felt that their world was perfect. They gathered around the piano together and sang carols of joy far into the night.